POKÉMON

Tree's a Crowd

**Adapted by
Tracey West and
Katherine Noll**

OFFICIAL
Pokémon
MASTER'S
CLUB

SCHOLASTIC INC.

New York Toronto London Auckland Sydney
Mexico City New Delhi Hong Kong Buenos Aires

Published by Scholastic Inc.
90 Old Sherman Turnpike, Danbury, CT 06816.

ISBN 0-439-72156-3

First Scholastic Printing, December 2004

Ash and his friends were lost!
"It is your fault," May said to
her little brother, Max.
"No, it is your fault!" Max said.

"Do not fight," Brock said.

"We get lost all the time," Ash said. "We will find our way."

"*Pika, pika!*" Pikachu agreed.

Then Ash pointed to something in a tree. "It is a Treecko!" he yelled.

Ash used his Pokédex to find out about Treecko.

"Treecko are Grass Pokémon," said the Pokédex. "They are good climbers. They live in tall trees."

"I want to catch it," Ash said.
He threw a Poké Ball at Treecko.
"Go, Poké Ball!"

Treecko hit the ball back with
its tail.

May laughed. "Remember what
you taught me? You have to *battle*
Treecko before you can catch it!
Some Pokémon Master you are."

Ash turned red. "I guess I could not wait," he said.

"Ash, Treecko is getting away!" Brock called.

Ash and Pikachu ran after Treecko. Brock, May, and Max stayed behind.

But Ash was not looking where he was going. He tripped over a big tree root!

When he looked up, he saw a very big tree.

"Look, Pikachu," Ash said. "This tree is so big! But it looks sick."

Then Ash saw Treecko up in the big tree.

"Hey, come down!" Ash yelled. "Let's battle!"

"Treecko! Tree!"
Treecko cried and
jumped down
from the tree.
Bam! Treecko
hit Pikachu
with its tail.

Pikachu fell. But it got back up.
It ran at Treecko.

Ash did not know it, but Team Rocket was watching.

"That Treecko is a good fighter," said Jessie.

"We should catch it," said James.

"We can bring it to the Boss," said Meowth. "He will really like that!"

Pikachu and Treecko did not finish their battle.

A group of other Treecko came by. The leader of the group talked to Treecko.

Meowth understood what the
Treecko were saying.

"The leader wants that Treecko
to leave the tree,"
said Meowth.

"They say
the tree is sick. But
that Treecko grew up in the tree.
It does not want to leave."

Treecko did not listen to the leader.

"Tree! Tree!" said the little Grass Pokémon.

The leader gave up. The group of Treecko walked away.

Treecko looked sad. It ran away!
Ash wanted to chase it again.
But Pikachu had another idea.

"Pika! Pika!" Pikachu told Ash.

"You think Treecko will come
back?" Ash asked. "Then we will
wait for it."

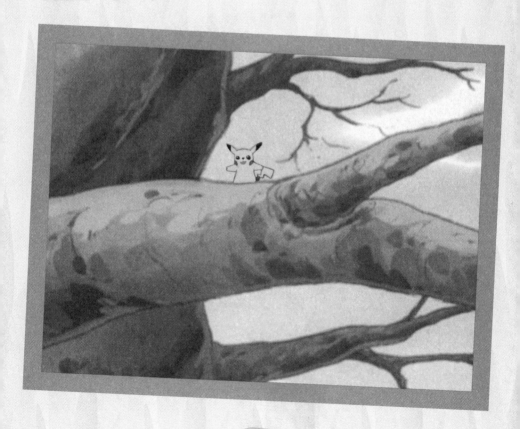

"Brock, May, and Max must be worried about us," Ash said. "I will send Taillow to find them."

Taillow came out of its Poké Ball. Then it flew away to find Ash's friends.

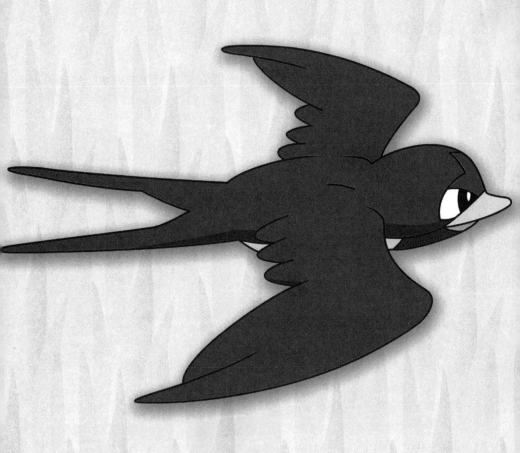

Ash and Pikachu waited.

Soon Treecko came back. It had a big leaf filled with water. It put the water on the roots of the tree.

"Treecko is trying to help the tree," Ash said.

Ash and Pikachu helped Treecko.
They got water for the tree, too.
"Tree! Tree!" said Treecko.
"You are welcome," said Ash.

Then Ash heard a noise. A big
machine came crashing through
the trees.

"It is Team Rocket!" Ash yelled.

The machine slammed into the trees. Lots of other Treecko fell out.

The machine scooped up the Treecko in nets. But it did not get the Treecko that took care of the sick tree.

Team Rocket put all of the other Treecko in a cage. They hooked the cage to their balloon. Then the balloon started to fly away.

"We are taking these Treecko to the Boss!" said Meowth.

"Pikachu! Stop them!" Ash yelled.
Pikachu shocked the balloon. But
the attack did not hurt the balloon.

"This balloon cannot be hurt by
Electric attacks!" James said.
Then Team Rocket grabbed
Pikachu in a net!

Treecko tried to
stop Team Rocket.
It shot a tree branch
at the balloon. But the
branch could not break
the balloon.

"Ha!" said Jessie.
"You cannot stop us!"

James threw out a Poké Ball.
Cacnea flew out.

Cacnea used Pin Missile. It shot
sharp spikes at Treecko.

But Treecko was fast! The spikes
missed it.

Then Treecko jumped into the
balloon basket and hit a button.
The cage opened. Pikachu and
all the other Treecko were free!

Treecko climbed onto the balloon. It made a face at Cacnea.

Cacnea got mad. It used Pin Missile again. The sharp spikes missed Treecko and broke the balloon! *Boom!* Team Rocket went blasting off. Treecko jumped down just in time.

"Treecko! Tree!" All of the Treecko were happy to be free. They became friends again.

But then something sad happened. The big tree split in two!

Treecko was very sad. But the tree left Treecko a seed.

With the seed, Treecko could grow a new tree.

Treecko wanted to finish the battle with Pikachu.

Brock, Max, and May came just in time.

Treecko and Pikachu battled.

Pikachu hit Treecko. Treecko jumped into the air.

Zap! Pikachu shocked it. Treecko fainted.

Ash threw his Poké Ball. This time, Treecko went inside.

"Electric attacks do not usually work on Grass Pokémon," Brock explained. "But Pikachu shocked Treecko in the air. That was a good move."

Ash let Treecko out of the ball. "Would you like to travel with us?" he asked.

"Treecko! Tree!" Treecko agreed. But first, it planted the seed in the ground. The other Treecko would care for the seed. Then Treecko waved good-bye to its friends.

It was ready for a new start with Ash and Pikachu!

Who's That Grass Pokémon?

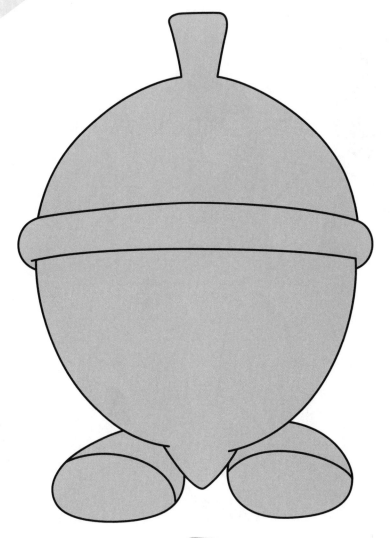

37

See page 45 for the answer.

Eye, Eye, Eye!

Can you tell who these Grass Pokémon are by just looking at their eyes?

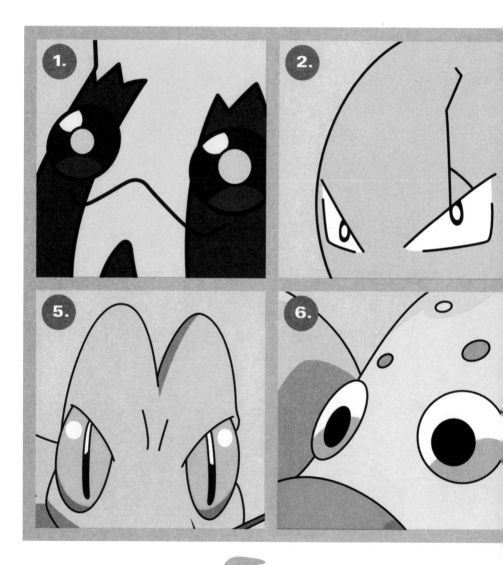

3.

4.

7.

8.

39

Check page 45 or your
Grass Pokédex for
the answers.

Battle Time!

Now it is your turn to battle! Read about each battle below. Then pick the best Pokémon to use against your opponent. In each battle, all of the Pokémon are the same level.

1. You are battling in the jungle. Your opponent throws out a Grovyle. Which of these Pokémon will do best against this Grass Type?

Huntail™
(Water)

Golbat™
(Poison/Flying)

Trapinch™
(Ground)

2. You are facing a Quilava with superhot Fire attacks. Which of these Pokémon will cool off Quilava?

Meganium™
(Grass)

Wailmer™
(Water)

Regice™
(Ice)

3. Your opponent chooses Donphan, a Ground Pokémon. Which one of these Pokémon will beat it?

Sceptile™
(Grass)

Plusle™
(Electric)

Registeel™
(Steel)

Check page 45 or your *Pokédex* books for the answers.

Pick the Grass/Poison Pokémon!

Look out! One of the Grass Pokémon in each row is also a Poison Type. The other two are not. Can you pick out the Grass/ Poison Pokémon in each row?

1. Bulbasaur™ Chikorita™ Treecko™

2. Cacnea™ Hoppip™ Oddish™

3. Sunflora™ Bellossom™ Roselia™

Nuzleaf™ **Venusaur**™ **Sceptile**™

Bellsprout™ **Shroomish**™ **Tangela**™

Exeggutor™ **Vileplume**™ **Cacturne**™

Meganium™ **Sunkern**™ **Ivysaur**™

43

Check page 45 or your *Grass Pokédex* for the answers.

Grass Pokémon Jokes

What do you call a Shroomish who knows how to have a good time?

A fun-gi!
(A fun "guy," get it?)

Why does Cradily live in salt water?

Because pepper makes it sneeze!

What do cars, elephants, and Exeggutors have in common?

They all have trunks!

What is a Tropius's favorite holiday song?

Jungle Bells!

Why couldn't Roselia ride its bike?

Because it lost its petals!

What did the Exeggcute say to the Exeggutor?

Let's get cracking!

Answers

Page 37: Who's That Grass Pokémon?
Seedot!

Pages 38–39: Eye, Eye, Eye!
1. Sunkern
2. Exeggcute
3. Bellossom
4. Bulbasaur
5. Treecko
6. Weepinbell
7. Nuzleaf
8. Cacturne

Pages 40–41: Battle Time!
1. Golbat (Poison/Flying beats Grass)
2. Wailmer (Water beats Fire)
3. Sceptile (Grass beats Ground)

Pages 42–43: Pick the Poison/Grass Pokémon!
1. Bulbasaur
2. Oddish
3. Roselia
4. Venusaur
5. Bellsprout
6. Vileplume
7. Ivysaur